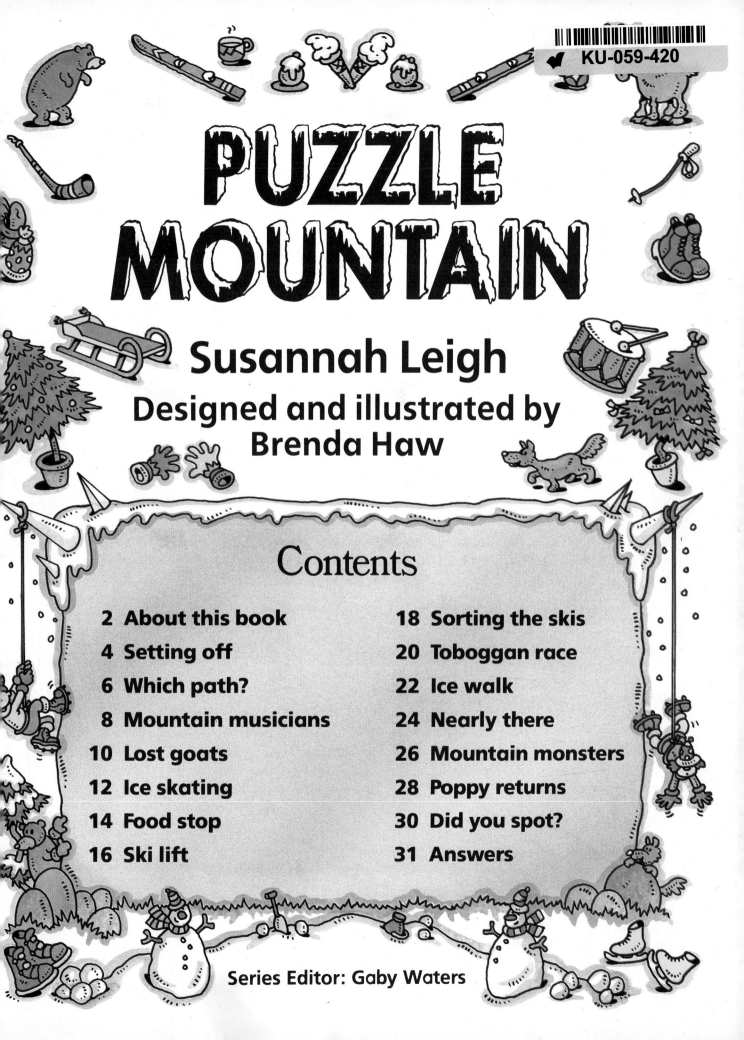

PUZZLE MOUNTAIN

Susannah Leigh

Designed and illustrated by Brenda Haw

Contents

Series Editor: Gaby Waters

About this book

This book is about a brave mountain climber called Poppy Pickaxe, her pet puppy, Bernard, and their adventures on Puzzle Mountain. You will find a puzzle on every double page. See if you can solve them all. If you get stuck, you can look at the answers on pages 31 and 32.

Poppy Pickaxe

Bernard

The people of Puzzle Mountain are having a sports day. Poppy is especially excited because today she will try to climb to the very top of Puzzle Mountain.
Read this poster to find out more.

Puzzle Mountain

CALLING ALL BRAVE MOUNTAIN CLIMBERS!

Can you climb to the very top of Puzzle Mountain?
There is a prize for the first person to get there.

Mountain legend has it that the rare Yodel flower grows on top of Puzzle Mountain.
Take a photo of the flower to prove you've reached the top - but don't pick it!

Yodel flower (artist's impression)

Everyone entering the climbing competition must wear a hat with a red ribbon.

No one has ever reached the very top of Puzzle Mountain before. The way up is difficult and sometimes dangerous. Will Poppy be the first to make it?

Things to spot.

The prizes for the sports day winners are missing. There is one prize hidden on every double page, except for pages 28 and 29. Look out for them. Here you can see all the prizes.

ski jumper on stand

prize badge

toboggan trophy

cowbell

red flag

golden pickaxe

ice skate necklace

little trumpet

mini ski pole

chocolate

hiking boot

snowman pendant

Basil
Basil collects rare mountain flowers. He wants to steal the Yodel flower. Watch out for him on every double page.

Mountain monster
People say that a strange, furry blue creature lives on Puzzle Mountain. Maybe you can spot him hiding on each double page.

3

Setting off

On the morning of her mountain climb, Poppy stepped out into the bustling village. High above her, far, far in the distance, loomed Puzzle Mountain.

Poppy wondered if the other climbers were as nervous as she was. Then she realized she didn't even know who they were. She remembered that everyone entering the climbing competition had to wear a red ribbon in their hat. Poppy looked around at all the people in the village. She soon spotted the other climbers.

There are eight other climbers. Can you spot them?

SKI SCHOOL

HOORAY FOR POPPY!

GOOD LUCK POPPY AND BERNARD

YUM

BUNS

SKI GEAR

I wonder if Basil's around?

7 PP

SALE

2 PP

4 PP

15 PP

BARGAIN BIN

Which path?

Poppy took one last look at the village. Then she called to Bernard, and the two friends bravely set off on their expedition.

Before long they arrived at six paths, all leading off in different directions. Only one path led right to the very peak of Puzzle Mountain. Poppy read the information board carefully. Then she looked at the signposts at the beginning of each path. She soon knew which one to take. She could even help the other hikers find their way.

Which path leads to the peak of Puzzle Mountain? Can you find the paths the others want?

Follow the signposts for:

HIKER'S HIGHWAY-

MOUNT LOFTY'S LANE -

WOODLAND WALK -

PUZZLE MOUNTAIN PEAK -

TRICKY TREK -

NUTTY NATURE TRAIL -

I'm looking for the Woodland Walk.

Which way to the Nutty Nature Trail?

Mountain musicians

Poppy bounded up the path. Soon she heard
spluttering noises, and saw an old man trying
to conduct a small band of musicians.

"Poppy!" he cried, turning around to face
her. "These are the Puzzle Mountain musicians.
They are trying to play their instruments, but
they are making some very strange sounds."

Suddenly, as the old man spoke, the sound of music started behind him. He spun around. The musicians were now playing their instruments perfectly! The old man turned to Poppy again. He was mystified. What had happened? Poppy looked at the musicians and saw six simple changes that had made all the difference.

Can you spot the differences?

Lost goats

Poppy waved goodbye to the old man and his band and climbed on, further up the mountain path. After a while, she met her friend Gretel the goatherd. Gretel was crying.

"Oh Poppy," she wailed. "The music from those mountain musicians has frightened my goats away. I've lost all seven of them. Can you see them? They are all brown with white faces."

Can you find Gretel's seven lost goats?

Ice skating

Leaving the sound of bleating goats behind her, Poppy scrambled along the mountain path. The route was getting steeper, and the air was colder. The path passed by the Puzzle Mountain ice rink, where the skating competition was about to start. The ice was full of people, but four of the contestants looked very glum.

TICKETS

ICE SKATING COMPETITION TODAY

The girls' partners are boys, and the boys' partners are girls.

"Can you help us, Poppy?" they called. "Our skating partners are on the ice somewhere, but we can't find them with all these other people here. Our partners' outfits match our own."

Can you find the four missing skaters?

Food stop

Poppy left the ice skaters and began climbing again, up towards the top of Puzzle Mountain. Soon she came to a small restaurant.

"We've helped a lot of people, Bernard," she said. "It's time we had a treat. Let's get something nice to eat."

Bernard woofed in agreement, and the two friends went inside. There were so many delicious things for sale, they didn't know what to choose. They both wanted something to eat, and to drink, but they only had ten Puzzle Pennies to spend between them.

What can Poppy buy to eat and drink, and what can she buy for Bernard to eat and drink, with just ten Puzzle Pennies?

Ski lift

Poppy licked the crumbs from her lips, and left the restaurant. She set off up the path once more, but stopped when she saw a group of eight grumpy looking skiers.

"We've got to take this ski lift to the other side of the mountain," grumbled the smallest skier. "But this notice has really confused us. Which chairs should each one of us use?"

"Everyone needs help today," thought Poppy as she read the big notice board.

Do you know which skier should use which chair?

Please read instructions before taking lift:

BLUE CHAIR - two adults only

RED CHAIR - one very tall person only

GREEN CHAIR - two adults with hats only

YELLOW CHAIR - cannot hold much weight

PURPLE CHAIR - two children only

We always travel together.

Sorting the skis

Poppy couldn't take the ski lift. She had to continue on the mountain path. She puffed and panted her way up. Before long, she bumped into her friend Tim, who was looking at a line of skis stuck into the snow.

"I am in the skiing competition today," he said. "But I can't find my speedy racing skis. I know they are the only matching pair here."

Can you find Tim's matching skis?

I can see two ski poles that match each other.

SKIING
COMPETITION
HERE

Toboggan race

Dodging the skiers, Poppy pressed on. A little higher up the mountain, she came across a toboggan race that was just about to start. The team that finished the course in the fastest time would be the winner. The three toboggan teams thought the course was very easy, but Poppy wasn't so sure.

"Be careful," she warned. "There are plenty of obstacles and dead ends along the way. Look out for them."

Can you find the clear route from the start to the finish of the race?

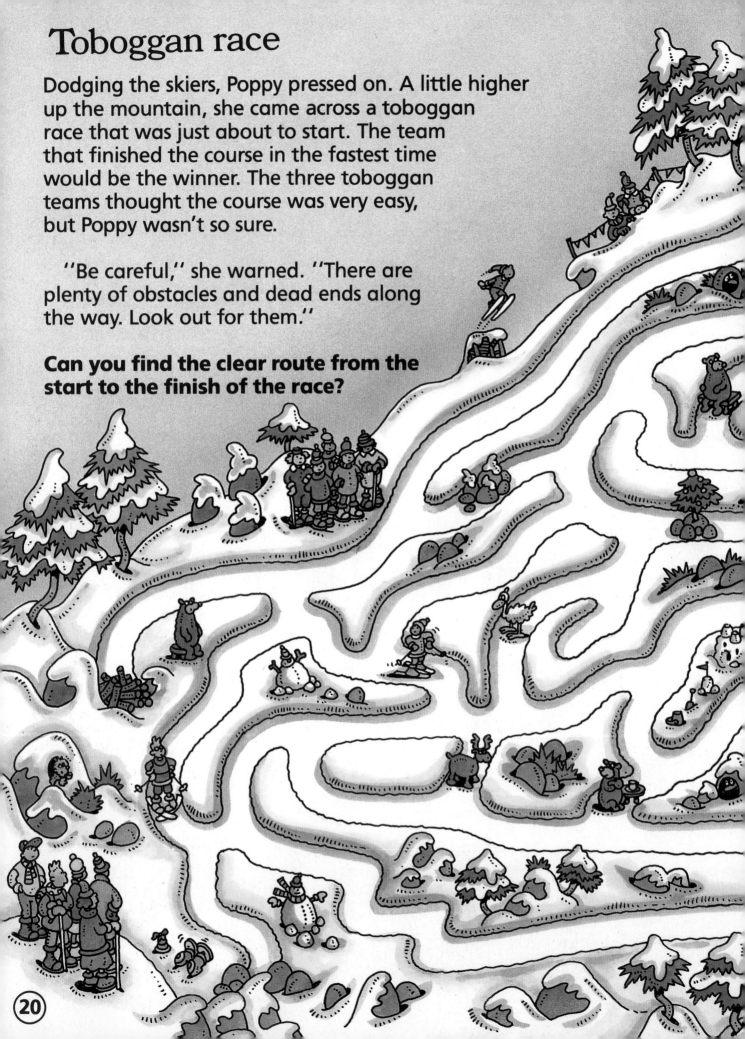

Ice walk

Poppy waved goodbye to the toboggan teams and carried on, climbing higher and higher up Puzzle Mountain. Soon there were no more people around, the mist was coming down, and Poppy and Bernard were on their own. They slid across the slippery ground. As they turned a corner, they stopped and gasped.

In front of them was the strangest glacier Poppy had ever seen. Beyond it, towered the very top of Puzzle Mountain. They were nearly there! But first they had to cross the ice, avoiding the deep pools and broken planks. There were two large notices on the glacier. Poppy peered at them through her blizzard-proof binoculars.

To get safely across the glacier, feed the wild snow bears with the six ice cream cones you'll find on the way.

Watch out for WOLVES. They don't eat ice cream.

She couldn't quite believe what she read. Wild snow bears and wolves? She hadn't expected this at all. It was going to be a dangerous journey...

Can you find the safe route across the glacier, picking up the six ice cream cones as you go?

Nearly there

Poppy skidded and slithered across the last of the ice. She landed with a crunch on the snowy bank on the other side of the glacier. Looking up ahead, she could see the peak of Puzzle Mountain, poking through the cloudy mist.

"Follow me, Bernard," she said. And the two friends began the final climb, upward and onward.

The way up was steep and very dangerous.

They hid from huge snowballs.

The air got thinner, and it was difficult to breathe. But at last the mist began to clear...

Poppy was amazed to see spikes of ice rising out of the mountain. Even more surprising were the holes, almost like windows, carved into the icy spikes. Then she spotted something she had only seen a picture of before. She had reached the very top of Puzzle Mountain.

What has Poppy spotted?

Mountain monsters

Click! Poppy took a photo of the Yodel flower. All at once, a huge hairy hand grabbed her arm and pulled her backwards. Poppy blinked, and in a flash she realized she was standing inside a room in a strange ice house. Three blue creatures were looking at her. Poppy rubbed her eyes. She was staring at a family of Puzzle Mountain monsters! Just then, a smaller monster rushed into the room and began to speak.

"I'm sorry I scared you Poppy," said the biggest monster. "But I am the guardian of the Yodel flower and I must protect it. It is the only one in the world, you know. Now I expect you want to get back to the sports day celebrations. Take my super-speedy red toboggan. It will get you down the mountain in no time — if I can find it."

Where is the super-speedy red toboggan?

Poppy returns

Night was falling as Poppy clambered on board the super-speedy red toboggan. She waved goodbye to her new friends, and with a whoosh she and Bernard were off, whizzing down the other side of Puzzle Mountain.
As they sped on, Poppy caught a glimpse of Basil, looking very scared. Perhaps now he would think twice before stealing any more mountain flowers.

Can you spot Basil?
Who is scaring him?

Don't tell anyone about us, Poppy!

Bye!

WELL DONE POPPY AND BERNARD

PRIZE SNOWBALL

snowmen love Poppy

HOOR

28

Did you spot?

Poppy reached the top of Puzzle Mountain first, and won a golden pickaxe! But whatever happened to the other eight competitors? How far did they get?

Below, you can see pictures of the other climbers, and read a little more about them. Now look back carefully through the book and see if you can spot them all.

Lady Cicily
She is clumsy, and rather accident prone.

Hungry Harry
He is always hungry and eats anything and everything.

Fred Photo
He likes mountain climbing – and photography.

Friendly Flora
She likes to stop and chat with her friends.

Lazy Larry
The fresh mountain air may make this sleepy climber drowsy.

Daredevil Dot
Her daredevil activities can be dangerous.

Fisher Jim
He enjoys climbing, but sometimes he'd rather be fishing.

Katy Climber
She wears baggy trousers, which may trip her up.

Answers

Pages 4-5 Setting off

The other mountain climbers are circled in red.

Pages 6-7 Which path?

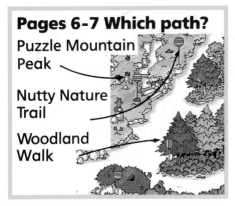

Puzzle Mountain Peak

Nutty Nature Trail

Woodland Walk

Pages 8-9 Mountain musicians

The differences are circled in red.
Can you find the extra differences?

Pages 10-11 Lost goats

The seven missing goats are circled in red.

Pages 12-13 Ice skating

The missing skating partners are circled in red.

Pages 14-15 Food stop

Poppy buys a pastry for two Puzzle Pennies, and a glass of juice for three Puzzle Pennies. For Bernard she buys a tasty bone for two Puzzle Pennies, and a bowl of doggy drink, for three Puzzle Pennies. This adds up to ten Puzzle Pennies exactly.

Pages 16-17 Ski lift

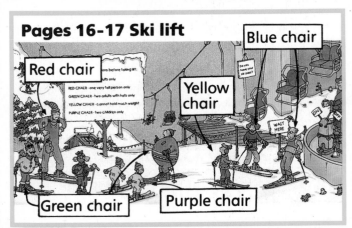

Blue chair

Red chair

Yellow chair

Green chair

Purple chair

Pages 18-19 Sorting the skis

These are Tim's matching skis.

These are his poles.

Pages 20-21 Toboggan race

The clear route from the start to the finish of the race is shown in red.

Pages 22-23 Ice walk

The six ice cream cones are circled in red. The safe route across the glacier is shown in black.

Pages 24-25 Nearly there

Poppy has spotted the Yodel flower.

Pages 26-27 Mountain monsters

The super-speedy red toboggan is here.

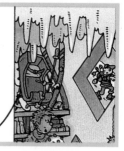

Pages 28-29 Poppy returns

The monster is scaring Basil!

Did you spot everything?

Sports day prizes

The chart below shows you which sports day prize is hidden on which double page.

Basil

Puzzle Mountain monster

Basil and the monster

Did you remember to watch out for Basil, and for the Puzzle Mountain monster? Look back through the book and see if you can spot them on each double page.

First published in 1993 by Usborne Publishing Ltd., Usborne House, 83-85 Saffron Hill, London EC1N 8RT, England.

Copyright © 1993 Usborne Publishing Ltd.

The name Usborne and the device ⊕ are Trade Marks of Usborne Publishing Ltd.

Printed in Portugal. UE